Tricky Rabbit

A Story from Cambodia to Read and Tell

Retold by Martha Hamilton and Mitch Weiss

Illustrated by Pat Paris

Richard C. Owen Publishers, Inc.
Katonah, New York

Every day a woman walked
home from the market
with a big basket of bananas
on her head.

She always went right past Rabbit's house.
The villagers warned the woman to take
a different path. They knew that Rabbit loved
to play tricks and cause trouble.

The woman did not like to take advice from anyone
so she ignored the villagers' warning.

3

Now, Rabbit loved bananas and was determined
to get them from the woman.

One day, he came up with a plan.

Rabbit lay down in the middle of the road and pretended to be dead.

When the woman passed by and saw him she thought, "Mmm. My family will have rabbit stew for dinner tonight."

She picked Rabbit up, threw him into her basket, and headed home.

While the woman dreamed of rabbit stew, Rabbit stuffed himself with her bananas.

When the woman got home, she took the basket off her head. Rabbit jumped out and scampered away.

All that was left in the basket were banana peels.

The woman was furious!
"That tricky Rabbit!" she cried.

After that, the woman paid attention
to what the villagers said.

And she never walked past Rabbit's house again.